D1266720

THE AMAZING ADVENTURES OF SUPERMAN!™

Alien Superman!

by YALE STEWART

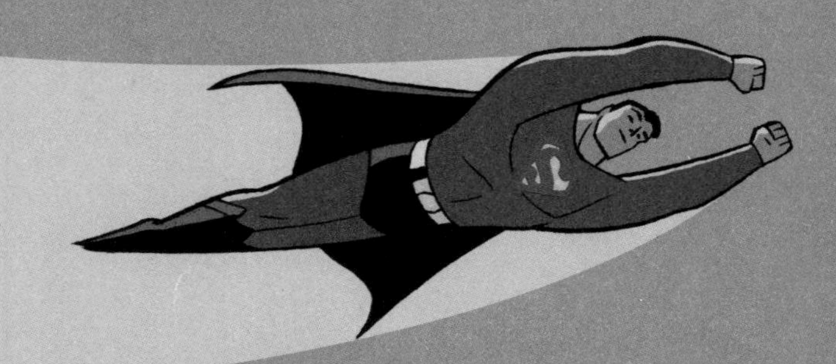

Superman created by Jerry Siegel and Joe Shuster
by special arrangement with the Jerry Siegel family

PICTURE WINDOW BOOKS
a capstone imprint

The Amazing Adventures of Superman
is published by Stone Arch Books
a Capstone Imprint
1710 Roe Crest Drive
North Mankato, Minnesota 56003
www.capstonepub.com

STAR32424

Cataloging-in-Publication Data is available at the Library of Congress website.
ISBN: 978-1-4795-5733-2 (library binding)
ISBN: 978-1-4795-5737-0 (paperback)

Summary: When the MAN OF STEEL suddenly changes into a strange, green creature at the hands of Lex Luthor, can even WONDER WOMAN take down the . . . Alien Superman?

Editor: Donald Lemke
Designer: Bob Lentz

Printed in the United States of America in Stevens Point, Wisconsin.
032014   008092WZF14

TABLE OF CONTENTS

Born among the stars.
Raised on planet Earth.
With incredible powers,
he became the
World's Greatest Super Hero.
These are...

Chapter 1

A TRAP

Inside a Metropolis skyscraper, Superman and Wonder Woman chase Lex Luthor. The evil businessman dives into a room and locks the door behind him.

"He's trapped!" shouts Wonder Woman.

With super-strength, Superman kicks down the steel door. WHAM!

Lex stands in the empty room. The room does not have any windows or doors.

"Looks like we've chased you to a dead end, Luthor," says Superman, smiling.

Lex pulls a high-tech remote control from his suit pocket. "You didn't chase me here, Superman," Lex replies. "I led you here!"

Lex presses a button on the remote. **BEEP.**

A red gas pours into the room from the ceiling vents. A thick cloud quickly fills the air. The heroes cough and sneeze.

Suddenly, the air clears. Wonder Woman grabs Lex. "Nice try," she says. "But a little gas won't stop us."

"Speak for yourself," says Lex, pointing behind her.

Chapter 2

ALIEN HERO

Wonder Woman spins around. The super hero can't believe her eyes.

"Superman?" she asks. The Man of Steel has become a . . . GREEN ALIEN!

“What have you done?” Wonder Woman asks Lex.

“I’ve created a new Red Kryptonite gas,” he replies. “It’s changed Superman into a monster!”

Then, a scream echoes from outside the building. Someone is in trouble!

Superman crashes through a wall. He flies to the street below. WHOOSH!

Superman spots a car that has crashed. People are trapped inside.

The hero tries using his heat vision to free them. He freezes the car instead!

Then Superman tries removing the door with his super-strength. When he touches the metal, the door melts away. His powers have gone haywire!

Meanwhile, Wonder Woman finds a steel beam. She wraps up Lex in a dozen metal knots.

"I'll be back for you," she says. Then she flies outside.

On the street, people scream. They run away from the alien monster.

"It's me!" shouts the Man of Steel. "Superman!"

Chapter 3

WELCOME BACK

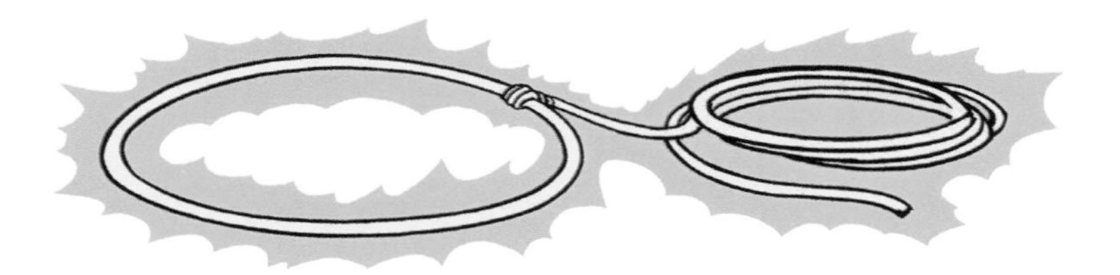

Wonder Woman removes the Lasso of Truth from her belt. "I hate to do this," she tells Superman. "But it's for your own good."

With a flick of her wrist, the lasso flies through the air. The rope twirls around Superman. Wonder Woman pulls the hero toward her.

Wonder Woman wraps Superman in her lasso. The Man of Steel is worn out by the gas. He falls asleep.

"Sweet dreams," Wonder Woman says.

Moments later, the super heroes arrive at the Fortress of Solitude. The secret hideout is filled with gadgets. But only time will heal the Man of Steel.

The next morning, sun shines through the icy walls of the Fortress of Solitude.

"Sleep well?" a voice asks Wonder Woman.

The sleeping hero's eyes open. "Superman!" shouts

Wonder Woman, seeing her friend.

"How did we get here?" asks the Man of Steel.

Wonder Woman explains everything to Superman.

"Did I hurt anyone?" he asks, worried.

"No," she replies, "but I'm glad you're back to normal."

Superman blasts a nearby metal chair with his heat vision. It melts into a red-hot puddle.

"My powers are back, too," says Superman.

"Do your powers include untying knots?" she asks.

Superman smiles and says, "Sounds like another amazing adventure awaits!"

4
BREAKING NEWS
4

SUPERMAN'S SECRET MESSAGE!

Hey, kids! When a problem is too big, what's the best thing to ask for?

Use the code below to solve the secret message!

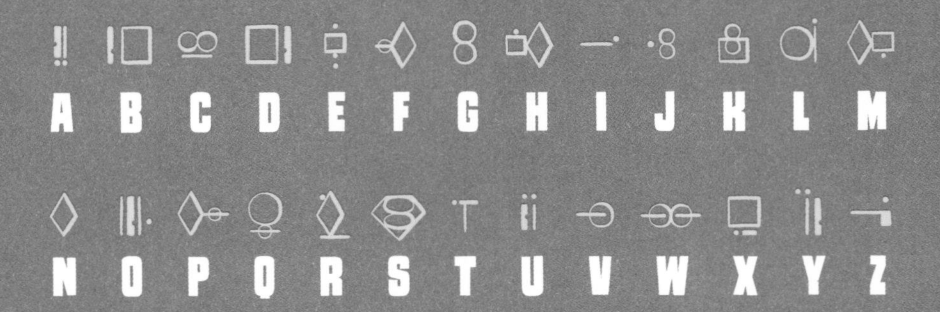

dead end (DED END)—a place without an exit

gadget (GAJ-it)—a small tool that does a particular job

haywire (HAY-wire)—acting wildly or out of control

hideout (HIDE-out)—a secret base where someone can hide

lasso (LASS-oh)—a length of rope with a large loop at one end that can be thrown over an object to catch it

skyscraper (SKYE-skray-pur)—a very tall building

THE AMAZING ADVENTURES OF SUPERMAN!™

COLLECT THEM ALL!

only from . . . **PICTURE WINDOW BOOKS**

YALE STEWART

Yale Stewart is an independent comic book artist, working primarily on his creator-owned project, "Gifted." His day job is working in the vintage clothing industry. He attended Savannah College of Art and Design and graduated with a BFA in Animation. Originally from St. Louis, MO, he currently resides in Savannah, GA. He is also an avid movie-watcher and music-listener, and eagerly awaits every baseball season.